POLLY-TASTIC
Adventure ™

Adapted by Justine Fontes
Illustrated by MADA Design, Inc.

Manufactured and printed in China.
ISBN: 978-0-696-23647-1

We welcome your comments and suggestions.
Write to us at: Meredith Books, Children's Books,
1716 Locust St., Des Moines, IA 50309-3023.
Visit us online at: meredithbooks.com

Meredith® Books
Des Moines, Iowa

Hidden objects by page number: 3. spine of book; 4. inside box; 5. in painting; 6. on Shani's dress; 7. in Lea's hand; 8. on podium; 9. on statue base; 10. below globe; 11. on Polly's helmet; 12. spine of book; 13. side of boat; 14. on vender's necklace; 15. on awning; 16. on shield; 17. on drum; 18. on center pillar (and in center of room); 19. on torch; 20. on pink vase; 21. on boat; 22. on vase; 23. on Shani's drum; 24. on vase

Polly Pocket and her peeps are totally stoked! Shani is starring as Queen Cleopatra in the class play, and they're all going to Egypt as part of a school cruise.

Before boarding, the girls spend a wonderful weekend in London at the Pocket Estate. In the totally awesome library, the friends find an ancient-looking book with a note about a hidden treasure from Polly's mom, whose passion was ancient Egypt. The book also contains a mysterious map with a missing corner.

"Dear Polly, this ancient tome holds great secrets and great danger. Hidden in its pages is the timeless key to a treasure beyond your wildest dreams. I was not able to complete the journey myself, but I hope you can follow my guiding light to finish what I began. I love you. Mom."

The treasure hunt begins in her mom's old office. Polly and her friends find a strange-looking box and a key. Inside are an old-fashioned compass and three small portraits of women in gowns.

Onboard the cruise ship, the girls spot paintings in the lobby, including one with the same kind of old-fashioned compass. Beth gets suspicious when she catches them studying the painting carefully—*too* carefully. There must be a reason. So while she watches Polly, Chrissy, and Lea, Beth tells her friends Tori and Evie to . . .

. . . spy on Shani and Lila, who are checking out the ship's costume room. As they had hoped, the girls find a gown like the ones in the oval portraits. Lila reads the label. "It's from the English Renaissance," she says.

Shani is puzzled. "That's like 1,500 years after Cleopatra lived, and England is a long way from Egypt."

Tempted by all the gorgeous clothes, the girls indulge their passion for fashion.

Later the friends
research the paintings.
"They're by Johannes Wynn, a Renaissance painter
known for his nautical-themed works and for his devotion
to his hobby—Egyptology!" Shani exclaims. "His best three
canvases are in the Louvre Museum in Paris."
Lea looks at the schedule. "That's where we'll be tomorrow!" she says.

At the Louvre the friends sneak away from the group. Polly, Lea, and Crissy find the three Wynn paintings. Crissy spots the three women—the same ones in the oval portraits—all holding urns.

"What do you think it means?" Lea asks.

Polly notices a clue. "The urns have the same shape as the map's missing corner!" she says.

Meanwhile, Shani and Lila disguise themselves as tour guides to get into a special Egyptian exhibit. The real guide says, "This is a statue of the goddess Hathor. She often appears as a woman with horns, but she is sometimes shown as a cow."

The girls travel to Rome, where Polly makes a rubbing of a monument. That night she compares it to the carving on the box. Shani exclaims, "That's the Lighthouse of Alexandria!"

"That's on our schedule for tomorrow," says Lila.

Shani corrects her. "The site is. The lighthouse no longer exists, but in Cleopatra's time, it was the tallest building on the planet."

The next day Polly's butler, Samuel, leads a parasailing tour of the coastline, while their teacher, Miss Marklin, takes a group to the marketplace. Polly's tether breaks and she flies free! High above the beach, Polly sees a stone shaped like a cow's head. Meanwhile, Shani finds a clue too: a statue of the Lighthouse of Alexandria with an eye of Hathor on top. The seller explains, "The goddess was also known as 'The Eye.'"

11

Shani and Polly both come to the same conclusion. "The lighthouse is the missing part of the map!" they exclaim.

But when Shani compares ancient and modern maps of Alexandria, she discovers that things aren't so simple. "Earthquakes have changed the coast," she reports sadly. "Much of the old city is underwater. The treasure is probably under the sea too."

Beth only overhears the part about the lighthouse. Determined to beat them to the treasure, she swipes the book while Polly and the Pockets rehearse for their concert.

The next day, both Beth and the map are missing. Polly and her friends quickly realize that Beth is in danger! Polly grabs the old compass, and the girls take a small boat to look for her.

The sky darkens. The compass spins wildly. And suddenly a huge wave swamps the boat! Then just as suddenly, the mist is pierced by a bright light from—the Lighthouse of Alexandria! Polly exclaims, "It's amazing!" just before another wave knocks the compass out of her hands.

On shore the girls see ancient Alexandrians. Then Crissy says, "Look at us!"

Polly nods, "That's why the map was of ancient Alexandria. The treasure is back in time, and the compass guided us here. This would have been my mom's dream come true."

The girls soon discover they can speak ancient Egyptian, or at least that's how their words sound to the natives. Shani is thrilled. "Look—an ancient bazaar! We have to check it out. Maybe we'll even see Cleopatra!"

The bazaar is full of way-cool stuff, like pottery and jewelry. Best of all, they make a frisky new friend, a funny little monkey they name Alex.

Then the blare of trumpets announces the approach of a royal party. Shani hopes to see Queen Cleopatra. Instead . . . it's Beth! "Intruders! Seize them!" Beth commands.

Polly and her peeps take off on a wild chase through the bazaar. Suddenly, a skinny man grabs them and says, "You're late! They're waiting." He pushes ancient instruments into the girls' hands and shoves them on stage. Crissy panics. "What do we do?" she cries.

Shani grabs a drum and begins a truly rocking beat. The other Pockets join in, and the crowd goes crazy! Beside Beth, a mysterious woman also enjoys the music. Her guards bring the girls to a palace where they meet Queen Cleopatra!

Beth tries to convince the queen that her new visitors can't be trusted. But Shani's cool head and hot drums impressed Cleopatra. The queen wants to give the band a tour of her town.

At Alexandria's famous library, Cleopatra explains what makes the city so great. "Every culture offers something vital," she says. "Alexandria is a place where we become brighter by bathing in the light of each other's differences."

That's it! Polly realizes. "That's the light my mom wanted to bring back. That's the treasure!"

When Crissy worries about getting stuck in ancient times, Lila replies, "I bet the book will show us the way home."

While Shani has dinner with Beth and Cleopatra, the others steal back the book and take it to the lighthouse. When Polly holds the book near a torch, a message written in invisible ink appears!

The message says, "All voyagers must return by the first full moon or be trapped forever."

"The full moon?" Lila exclaims. "We only have a few hours!"

Polly rereads her mom's note. Certain phrases—"the timeless key to a treasure" and "follow my guiding light"—suddenly make sense. Polly follows the lighthouse's beacon to a keyhole-shaped patch of light on the sea. "That's where we need to sail—and soon!" she says.

The girls hurry back to the palace to get Shani and Beth. But Shani isn't sure she wants to go home. "Cleopatra asked me to become a member of her court!" she beams.

Polly persuades Shani to return to where she belongs. And the queen sweetly accepts the gift of their furry friend. "I promise little Alex will be in good hands," she says.

Beth fumes when Cleopatra tells her to go home with the other girls.

When they reach the keyhole-shaped patch of light, a huge wave once again swamps the boat. Soon Crissy spots the cruise ship and exclaims, "We're back!" Lila notices that they are now in modern clothes. Beth looks down at herself and cries, "My jewels! That's it. Give me back the book. I'm going back to the palace."

But Polly's hands are empty. "The book's gone," she says. "It must have vanished when we returned to the present."

The girls arrive just in time to change into their costumes for the full moon dance on deck. Before their first song, Polly says, "Hey, everyone! We're Polly and the Pockets and we've had an incredible journey." Only Polly and her peeps know that she doesn't mean the cruise.

"We've been inspired by Alexandria's example of bringing all cultures together. In that spirit, I'd like to dedicate the Emily Pocket Library of Alexandria, a new group with the goal of putting books in the hands of kids all over the world. To start the collection, I'm donating my personal library."

While everyone else cheers, Samuel wipes away a proud tear.

"So let's rock the house!" Polly goes on. Then she turns to Shani. "Take it!"

Just as she did in ancient Alexandria, Shani starts a groovy beat that soon has everyone dancing happily.

Polly and her friends decide not to tell anyone about their time traveling adventure. "No one would believe us anyway," Crissy muses. But the pictures on an ancient vase prove that some things, like friendship and music, are eternal.